Mail Order Muse

Book Fifty in the Brides of Beckham

Kirsten Osbourne

Chapter One

Diana Westcott stood at the window of her Beckham, Massachusetts home, her deep blue eyes scanning the lush gardens that surrounded the estate. The sun was setting, casting a warm glow over the manicured lawns and well-tended flower beds. Despite the beauty before her, Diana's heart felt heavy with an unshakable sense of loneliness.

Diana had inherited this grand residence and a sizable fortune from her recently deceased parents. In the wake of their tragic passing, she found herself grappling with the weight of their legacy and the unwanted attention it brought her.

"Miss Westcott?" called Esther, the housekeeper, as she entered the room. "You have another suitor waiting for you in the drawing room."

"Thank you, Esther," Diana replied with a sigh, her delicate features reflecting her mounting frustration. "Please, give me a moment to collect myself."

It seemed every man in Beckham sought her hand in marriage, but their intentions were transparent—they desired her wealth and social standing, not the love she yearned to give and receive.

"Is there no one who can see past my fortune?" she whispered to herself, her fingers absently tracing the embroidery on her silk gown.

"Miss Westcott, if I may," began Esther hesitantly. "You deserve better than these men who only see your wealth. Perhaps it is time to explore other possibilities."

"Other possibilities?" Diana's eyes narrowed as she turned to face the older woman.

"Forgive me for speaking out of turn, Miss," Esther said, lowering her gaze. "But ever since your parents passed, you've been hoping to find love, and all these suitors have brought you nothing but disappointment."

"Maybe you're right," Diana admitted, her voice tinged with sadness. "But what choice do I have?"

"Perhaps there is another way to find love, Miss Westcott. A way where your wealth won't be the center of attention."

Diana's eyes flickered with curiosity, and she asked, "What do you mean, Esther?"

"Promise me you'll think about it, dear," Esther said gently, a knowing smile gracing her lips.

"Very well," Diana replied, her determination resolute. "I promise."

As she descended the grand staircase to face yet another suitor, Diana couldn't help but wonder if there was a path that would lead her to the love she so desperately sought—a love founded on genuine connection and not the shallow allure of her inheritance.

The following day, Diana stepped into the bustling post office. The social scene in Beckham had become stifling, and she desperately longed for a genuine connection amidst the superficial chatter that filled her days.

"Miss Westcott!" called a friendly voice. Diana turned to see Elizabeth Tandy, a well-respected matchmaker in town. She was a petite woman with kind eyes and a warm smile that immediately put others at ease.

"Mrs. Tandy," Diana replied, returning the smile. "How are you today?"

"Quite well, thank you," Elizabeth said, stepping closer. "And yourself? I haven't seen you at any gatherings lately."

"Truth be told, I've grown weary of the local events," Diana admitted. "It seems all anyone wishes to discuss is my inheritance, not who I am as a person."

"Ah, yes," Elizabeth nodded sympathetically. "I can imagine how tiresome that must be. You know, there are other ways to find love, Miss Westcott."

"Such as?" Diana asked, curiosity piquing.

"Have you ever considered becoming a mail-order bride?" Elizabeth suggested gently. "There are many men in the western states looking for wives, and they care more about finding a true partner than about wealth."

Diana's eyes widened, the possibility washing over her like a wave of fresh air. A new start, a place where her fortune wouldn't define her—could it really be possible?

"A mail-order bride?" she echoed, her mind racing with questions. "Wouldn't that be...risky?"

"Of course, there are always risks when venturing into the unknown," Elizabeth conceded. "But think of the rewards. A chance to find true love, someone who cherishes you for who you are, not for your money."

Diana weighed the idea, her heart pounding in her chest. It was certainly a bold move, but one that could ultimately lead her to the life she so desperately craved.

"Would you help me, Mrs. Tandy?" Diana asked, determination shining in her eyes.

"Absolutely," Elizabeth replied with a reassuring smile. "You deserve happiness, Miss Westcott, and I will do everything in my power to help you find it."

"Thank you," Diana whispered, feeling as though a great weight had been lifted. As she left the post office, her steps felt lighter, her heart filled with hope. For the first time in what seemed like an eternity, Diana dared to believe that a genuine connection—and true love—might finally be within her grasp.

Later at home, Diana's heart raced with equal parts excitement and trepidation, her fingers tracing the delicate curve of her mother's silver locket that hung around her neck. The decision to travel west had been made, and it seemed there was no turning back now.

"Can I really find love so far from home?" she wondered, her anxious thoughts darting like shadows in the firelight. "What if none of the men can see past my fortune?"

"Could this be the path to finding someone who loves me for who I am?" Diana whispered into the mirror, searching her own eyes for assurance. "I won't let fear hold me back. I deserve happiness."

The following morning, Diana set out for Elizabeth Tandy's home, just down the street from her own. She bundled up well, in a white coat, hat, scarf, and mittens, knocking on the door to the older woman's home.

Elizabeth's husband Bernard came to the door, and smiled with a nod. "Miss Westcott, Elizabeth said you may be stopping by soon."

He opened the door wide. "My wife is in her office. Last door on the left. Please inform her that I'll be in with tea and cookies in a moment."

Diana took the few steps to Elizabeth's office and knocked on the open door. "Mr. Tandy said to let you know he'll be in with tea and cookies in a moment."

Elizabeth's face lit up in a smile. "Diana, come in! Call me Elizabeth please."

Diana started to tell Elizabeth to use her own first name, but she realized the other woman already had. She sat down on the sofa Elizabeth waved her toward. "I've decided I want to be a mail-order bride, but I don't want my future husband to know about my money. Not until I decide to tell him."

Elizabeth nodded. "I think that's a very smart decision." She started flipping through a stack of letters. "I thought about who would be a good match for you after we talked, and I think Kevin is the man you're looking for." Elizabeth pushed a letter toward Diana. "Tell me what you think."

Dear Madam,

I hope this letter finds you in good health and high spirits. My name is Kevin and I am writing to you from the vast, open plains of the great West. I work as a foreman on a bustling ranch, a position that fills my days with hard work and my heart with a deep sense of satisfaction. However, as the sun sets and the cattle retire for the night, I find myself longing for companionship, for someone to share the quiet moments and the grand adventures that life on this ranch offers.

I am not a man of many words, but I find comfort in the simplicity of life here. The land under the endless sky is a sight to behold, especially when the setting sun paints the sky with hues of red and gold. The rustling of the leaves and the distant sound of cattle are the symphony I fall asleep to each night. And yet, there's an emptiness that lingers, a silence that aches to be filled with shared laughter, soft whispers, and heartfelt conversations.

My boss recently found joy in marriage with a lovely lady from your parts, through the same matchmaker. Their happiness is palpable, filling the air with a warmth that makes even the coldest of winter days bearable. It is their shared contentment that inspires me to write to you today. I, too, yearn for such companionship, for a partner who would stand by my side through thick and thin, sharing in the triumphs and weathering the storms that life might throw our way.

I seek a wife to keep my house and cook my meals. But I also seek a friend, a confidante, a partner in every sense. I promise to provide a life of stability and simplicity, under the wide-open skies of the West. In return, all I ask for is honesty, companionship, and a willingness to embrace the life that awaits here.

I understand that leaving one's home to start a new life in an unfamiliar land is no small decision. I assure you, that should you choose to embark on this journey, you will find in me a man who respects your courage, values your companionship, and cherishes your presence.

Please take your time to consider my proposal. I eagerly await your response and the prospect of getting to know you better.

Yours sincerely,

Kevin Smythe

Diana read the letter once more and nodded. "I think he's what I'm looking for."

Elizabeth smiled. "I think he'll suit you nicely. If and when you tell him about your wealth is up to you, of course. And you'll find that you have a dear friend in Keri White, his boss's new bride. I implore you to set out to meet her as soon as you arrive."

"What do I do now?" Diana asked.

"How soon do you want to leave?" Elizabeth asked. "I could send a telegram and let him know you're on your way, or you could write a letter. With a telegram, you could leave tomorrow. With a letter, you'd want to wait for a response that would take at least twenty days or so."

Diana bit her lip as she considered. "I'll lose my nerve if I wait too long."

"I'll send a telegram then. When would you like to leave?"

Diana thought for a moment about all the things that must be done before she could go. Finally, she said, "I want to leave the day after tomorrow." She didn't have to do it all alone. She had servants who she would keep on at least for a few months until she knew if her marriage would work out.

Elizabeth smiled. "I'll send a telegram in the morning. I hope you plan on traveling in a sleeping compartment."

Diana nodded. "Are there people who don't?"

Elizabeth smiled. "Yes, there are."

"That's sad," Diana said shaking her head.

When she arrived home after having tea and cookies with Elizabeth, Diana told her housekeeper what she planned to do.

"Then we mustn't waste any time, dear," the housekeeper replied, her voice filled with warmth. "We'll start by packing your belongings and making arrangements for your departure."

Over the next two days, Diana's home became a whirlwind of activity as she carefully selected which cherished possessions would accompany her on her journey. She packed her favorite books, a handful of elegant gowns, and the delicate porcelain tea set that had belonged to her mother, each item a tangible reminder of the life she was leaving behind.

As Diana prepared to say goodbye to her friends and familiar surroundings, she was flooded with bittersweet emotions—sadness at leaving all that she had known, yet excitement for the new life that awaited her in the West.

"Promise me you'll write," her closest friend, Margaret, implored as they embraced one last time.

"Of course, I will," Diana reassured her, her own eyes brimming with tears. "And when I find the love I've been searching for, you'll be the first to know."

With her bags packed and her goodbyes said, Diana took one last look at the home that had sheltered her for so many years, its familiar walls now echoing with memories. And as she stepped out into the cool Massachusetts air, she felt the weight of her past lifting from her shoulders, replaced by a newfound sense of freedom and determination.

"Goodbye, Beckham," she whispered, her heart swelling with hope as she embarked on the journey that would change her life forever.

The brisk autumn air nipped at Diana's cheeks as she stood on the platform, her breath forming a delicate mist in front of her face. The train station bustled with activity, the cacophony of voices and clanking metal creating a symphony of anticipation. Heart pounding in her chest, Diana clutched the worn leather handle of her suitcase, her knuckles white from the intensity of her grip.

"Last call for the westbound train to Wyoming!" A conductor's voice rang out, slicing through the din like a knife. "All aboard!"

Diana hesitated for a moment, her emerald eyes scanning the crowd one last time as if seeking reassurance. She felt a gentle hand on her shoulder and turned to see Margaret standing beside her, a reassuring smile gracing her lips.

"Go on, Diana," Margaret urged softly. "Your destiny awaits."

"Thank you, Margaret," Diana whispered, her voice quivering with emotion. "I couldn't have made it this far without you."

"Remember," Margaret continued, her eyes glistening with unshed tears, "you are strong, brilliant, and deserving of love. Don't let anyone make you believe otherwise."

With a deep breath, Diana nodded, her resolve solidifying within her. Boarding the train, she was shown to her sleeper car. She thought she would spend the trip embroidering the apron her housekeeper had given her as a going-away gift. If one must wear an apron, it should be a pretty one.

It was the following morning when she was in the dining car, facing yet another meal alone. She should have been used to it, but did anyone truly ever get used to being all alone?

"Excuse me, miss?" A fellow passenger's voice interrupted Diana's reverie. "May I sit here?"

"Of course," Diana replied, happy for the company of the older woman.

"Thank you, dear," the woman said, settling into the seat across from Diana. "My name is Agnes. What brings you out west?"

"Love, I hope," Diana admitted, offering a tentative smile. "I'm seeking a man who will love me for who I am, not what I possess."

"Ah, a noble pursuit," Agnes nodded sagely. "You're wise to keep your wealth a secret. Too many people are blinded by greed."

"Exactly," Diana agreed, her determination only growing stronger. She knew that to find true love, she would have to be patient, discerning, and willing to risk it all for the promise of something greater.

"Here's to new beginnings," Diana whispered as she raised her glass in a toast with the older woman, so thankful not to be alone, if only for a meal.

As the train rattled westward, Diana's excitement and nervousness ebbed and flowed like the landscape outside her window. She spent hours gazing at the seemingly endless plains that stretched out before her, imagining the life that awaited her in Wyoming. Her thoughts drifted to the strong, capable man she hoped to find – someone who would truly appreciate her for who she was, not for the fortune she had so carefully hidden away.

"Excuse me, ma'am," the conductor announced, stepping into their car. "We'll be arriving in Wyoming soon."

Diana's heart raced at the words, her anticipation bubbling over as she quickly gathered her belongings. The train began to slow, and she pressed her face against the window.

As the train pulled into the station, Diana marveled at the sight before her. The bustling town seemed to teem with energy, its wooden storefronts and dirt streets promising adventure and opportunity. She stepped off the train, her boots sinking slightly into the soft earth as she breathed in the clean, crisp air.

Diana's heart swelled with hope as she took in her surroundings, the vast Wyoming landscapes stretching out in every direction, beckoning her to explore them.

This was it— her chance to start anew, to leave behind the shallow pursuits of her past and find a love that would endure the test of time.

Determination and hope coursed through her veins, filling her with renewed purpose as she took her first steps toward the life she had always dreamed of.

"Here's to new beginnings," she murmured, a soft smile playing on her lips.

Diana's heart pounded in her chest as she stepped off the train, the cool Wyoming breeze brushing against her cheeks and sending a shiver down her spine. Her eyes darted around the bustling platform, taking in the faces of those who had also arrived, each with their own story and reason for being there.

"Miss Diana?" a voice called out, snapping her back to reality. She turned to see a sweet woman, close to her own age, with kind eyes and a warm smile approaching her, extending a hand in greeting. "I'm Keri White, Harry's wife. We're so happy to have you here."

"Thank you," Diana replied, grasping Keri's hand firmly. "It's a pleasure to meet you. I must admit, I'm a bit nervous about all of this."

Keri chuckled softly and patted her hand reassuringly. "That's perfectly normal. But I have a feeling you're going to fit right in here. Harry and I came in with Kevin so you could meet him, and we could be there for the wedding."

"Really?" Diana's eyes widened. "That's...that's wonderful! Thank you so much."

"Of course," Keri said warmly. "Now, let's introduce you to your fiancé. Do you have a trunk?"

"I do," Diana responded.

"All right. Wait here, and I'll be right back."

Chapter Two

The sun was beginning to set as Diana stood nervously on the train platform, clutching her small suitcase tightly. The warm colors of the sky intermingled with the cool autumn breeze that brushed against her face, a stark contrast to the warmth of her racing heart. She had been waiting for this moment for weeks, and now that it was finally here, she could hardly believe it.

"Diana?" a friendly voice called out to her. As she turned, her eyes met those of Keri, who was approaching with a tall, broad-shouldered man in tow. Keri's smile was so welcoming that Diana couldn't help but feel drawn to her. "This is Kevin," she said, gesturing toward the man beside her.

"Hello," Kevin said, extending his hand for Diana to shake. His voice was deep and reassuring. There was something undeniably comforting about him.

"Hello," Diana replied, her voice wavering slightly as she took his strong hand in hers. As their fingers touched, she felt an unexpected jolt of electricity pass between them, making her heart skip a beat. She met Kevin's gaze, and in that moment, it seemed as if time itself had come to a standstill. For a few seconds, they were the only two people on the crowded platform, their eyes locked in a silent exchange of curiosity and intrigue.

"Nice to meet you, Diana," Kevin said softly, breaking the spell. A faint blush crept across his cheeks, and Diana realized that he must have felt the same spark of connection that she did.

"Likewise," she replied, her voice steadier now. She glanced down at the small suitcase she held and then back up at Kevin, wondering what the future held for them. It was a new beginning, and though she didn't know what would come next, she couldn't help but feel hopeful.

"Shall we?" Keri asked, gesturing toward the waiting carriage nearby. Kevin offered his arm to Diana, and with her heart pounding in her chest, she accepted. Together, they began their journey into the unknown, with the promise of a connection that felt as old as the mountains themselves guiding them forward.

The sun dipped low on the horizon, casting a golden glow over the quiet Wyoming town. As their carriage rattled along the cobblestone streets, Diana couldn't help but steal glances at Kevin, who sat across from her. She felt butterflies in her stomach, and she wondered if he shared her nervous excitement. "Tell me about yourself, Diana."

Diana hesitated, unsure of how much to reveal. "Well, I'm originally from Boston. My parents...they passed away recently." She paused for a moment, then forced a small smile. "I've always loved the idea of living out West, though. The wide-open spaces, the mountains...it calls to me."

Kevin nodded. "I can understand that. I was born and raised in Wyoming, and I wouldn't trade it for anything. There's just something about the land that gets into your soul, you know?"

"Exactly!" Diana exclaimed, feeling a sense of relief that he understood her longing to escape city life. "I want to be a part of something bigger, to work with my hands and make a difference, not just flit around in ballrooms like a social butterfly."

"Sounds like we have similar aspirations," Kevin said with a gentle smile. "I've worked on the White's ranch for years now. It's hard work, but there's nothing more rewarding than seeing the fruits of your labor come to life."

As they continued talking, Diana found herself drawn to Kevin's passion for his work and the way he spoke of the people and animals in his care. It reminded her of her own dreams of creating a meaningful life beyond the confines of wealth and society.

But as their conversation flowed, Diana became increasingly aware of the secret she held—her vast inheritance, tucked away in a bank account far from Wyoming. She longed to be honest with Kevin, but the fear of being loved only for her money gnawed at her. She had been deceived before, and she couldn't bear the thought of it happening again.

"Diana?" Kevin's voice brought her back to the present. "Is everything all right? You seem lost in thought."

"Ah, yes, sorry," she stammered, trying to regain her composure. "I was just thinking about how much I'm looking forward to this new chapter of my life."

"Me too," he said softly, reaching across the carriage to take her hand. His touch sent a shiver down her spine. "I think we're going to make a great team, Diana."

She smiled at him, her heart swelling with hope. And as they continued toward their shared future, she resolved to find the courage to face her fears and trust in the possibility of love—real, unconditional love—between them.

"Tell me about your family, Diana," Kevin said as he helped her into the buggy they were already in a carriage. He looked genuinely interested in her life, which made her feel valued. She hesitated for a moment, wondering how much she should share.

"Well, my parents were loving but very protective," she began, picking at the edge of her dress. "I had a wonderful childhood, but I always felt like there was something more out there, something bigger than the world they kept me in."

Kevin nodded, encouraging her to continue. "It sounds like you were craving adventure, wanting to see what else was out there."

"Yes, exactly! I've been searching for a place where I can truly be myself, without expectations or limitations." Diana's eyes sparkled with excitement as she spoke, revealing her passion for change.

"What about you? What was your childhood like?" she asked, turning the conversation toward him.

He took a deep breath, his gaze becoming distant as he recalled memories long buried. "Well, I grew up on a small farm in Wyoming. My father passed away when I was young, so it was just me, my mother, and my sister. We didn't have much, but we were happy."

"Did you always want to work on a ranch?" Diana inquired, curious about his dreams.

"Actually, no," Kevin admitted, rubbing the back of his neck. "When I was a kid, I used to dream of being a doctor, helping people who couldn't afford medical care. But times were tough, and I had to put those dreams aside to support my family."

Diana felt a pang of sadness for the sacrifices he had made but admired his devotion to his loved ones. "I think it's incredibly noble, what you've done for your family. And who knows? Maybe someday you'll be able to pursue that dream again."

"Maybe," he said with a small smile. "But right now, I'm just grateful to have this chance to start fresh with you."

Their eyes met, and in that moment of vulnerability, they shared an unspoken understanding. Both had faced obstacles and losses, and both longed for a new beginning where they could create a life filled with love and purpose. As he drove toward the church, her hopes were high. She wanted nothing more than a happy marriage.

She thanked God that Keri was there beside her, as she already felt comfortable with her new friend.

"Ready?" Keri whispered, linking arms with Diana as they walked down the aisle. The scent of wildflowers filled the air, mingling with the warm, earthy aroma of polished wooden pews. A simple affair, the wedding suited both Diana and Kevin's desires for intimacy.

"More than ever," Diana replied, her voice soft yet resolute. As she reached the altar, her eyes locked onto Kevin's. Deep inside her, she knew she was doing the right thing.

"Diana, do you take Kevin to be your lawfully wedded husband, to have and to hold, from this day forward?" the minister asked, his voice steady and comforting.

"I do," she answered, her voice unwavering.

"Kevin, do you take Diana to be your lawfully wedded wife, to have and to hold, from this day forward?"

"I do," Kevin responded with equal certainty.

"By the power vested in me, I now pronounce you husband and wife. You may kiss the bride."

As their lips met for the first time, Diana felt a surge of emotion fill her chest, a mixture of joy, relief, and anticipation for the days to come. In that moment, she knew that no matter what challenges lay ahead, she and Kevin were meant to be together.

Their wedding celebration was a modest, joyful gathering at the White's ranch, where friends and family toasted the newlyweds and shared in their happiness. As the sun dipped below the horizon, painting the sky a brilliant array of colors, Diana took a moment to stand back and absorb the beauty of her new home.

"Quite the view, isn't it?" Kevin said, coming up behind her and wrapping his arms around her waist.

"Stunning," she murmured, leaning into his embrace. The ranch sprawled out before them, the land stretching as far as the eye could.

"Welcome home, Diana," Kevin whispered into her ear, his breath warm against her skin. She closed her eyes, allowing herself to fully experience the sensation of belonging, of being loved not for her wealth but for who she was deep within.

"Thank you, Kevin," she replied. "Thank you for giving me a chance to begin anew."

Chapter Three

The Wyoming sun was setting as Diana and Kevin entered their modest home, the warm hues of twilight cascading through the windows and casting a soft glow across the floor. They were now a married couple, bound together by fate and the matchmaking of Elizabeth Tandy

"Kevin, where would you like me to put these books?" Diana inquired, her arms laden with books she had collected over the years.

"Anywhere you'd like," Kevin replied, looking up from the newspaper he was reading.

Diana's eyes scanned the room for a suitable spot to store her beloved books. She noticed that Kevin preferred a tidy and organized environment, with everything having its designated place. As she set about arranging her books on the shelf, Kevin caught sight of the beautiful artwork adorning the covers. He realized that his new bride had a deep love for both books and art, which intrigued him.

"Your collection is quite impressive, Diana," Kevin remarked, admiring the rows of colorful spines.

"Thank you," she said with a shy smile. "Books have always been my escape."

THE SOFT GLOW OF CANDLELIGHT flickered across the wooden walls of the cozy cabin, casting dancing shadows on the handcrafted furniture. Diana stood by the window, her dress pooled around her feet and took a deep breath.

"Are you all right?" Kevin's gentle voice came from behind her, his concern evident in every word. He had been so patient, so understanding since they began this unexpected journey together.

"Of course," Diana replied softly. There was something undeniably thrilling about finally having someone care for her well-being—even if it was a man she barely knew. Slowly, she turned to face him, trying to steady her nerves.

Kevin stood in the middle of the room, his tall, lean frame bathed in the warm candlelight. His strong hands fiddled with the buttons of his waistcoat, betraying his own apprehension. Yet, when he looked up and met her eyes, a gentle smile spread across his rugged features, easing some of the tension between them.

"Would you like help with your dress?" he asked hesitantly.

"Since it's already at my feet, probably not," Diana murmured. "I wouldn't mind help with my corset though." As he approached, she marveled at the way his brown eyes seemed to soften as they studied her.

Kevin carefully untied the strings on her corset, his fingertips brushing against her skin with a lightness that sent shivers down her spine. As the fabric fell away from her shoulders, Diana felt a surge of vulnerability—and yet, she also sensed that Kevin would do everything in his power to protect her.

She knew that this marriage was one of convenience, born out of necessity rather than love. But somehow, as she stood there in the dimly lit cabin, she couldn't help but feel that perhaps fate had brought them together for something greater.

"Let's make this night special," Kevin said softly.

As they came together, their bodies pressed close, Diana felt something inside her awaken. A passion, a desire for connection that she had never known before. And as they explored each other, their hearts beating in unison, she realized that this unexpected union might just be the beginning of a love story.

The following morning, after Kevin went to work, Diana continued to unpack and organize her belongings, making her own things fit around his. The foundation of their new life together had been laid – now it was time for them to build upon it, brick by loving brick.

When Kevin arrived home at the end of the day, he stood for a moment, looking at freshly unpacked stacks of books and paintings. Diana stood beside Kevin admiring her handiwork as she arranged her precious collection on the shelves that lined one wall of their shared living space. Kevin stood beside her, his gaze shifting between the organized rows of novels and the meticulously hung artwork.

"Your taste in literature and art is fascinating," he said.

As they discussed their preferences, Diana realized she'd forgotten to cook something for supper. "I didn't cook!" she said, with her eyes wide. She'd made pancakes for breakfast, but it was truly the only thing she knew how to make. "I'm so sorry! I'll start the pancakes in a moment."

He looked at her as she hurried away from him. "Pancakes again?"

"It's all I know how to cook. Someone needs to get me a receipt book for Christmas!"

Kevin stared at her. Christmas was still two weeks away. She wasn't going to start learning to cook for two weeks? By then, he'd have pancakes coming out his ears.

"Perhaps you should go to Keri's house and spend some time with her. She's an excellent cook."

Diana frowned. "I suppose I can't expect to feed you pancakes for every meal for two weeks. I'll go see her tomorrow."

Kevin smiled. "I'd appreciate that."

"KERI!" DIANA CALLED as she rushed to the main ranch house. She knocked on the door, calling her friend's name again.

"Yes," Keri replied, opening the door wide. She wore a kind smile that made Diana feel at ease. "What's on your mind?"

"Kevin and I have been talking, and I've decided that I want to learn how to cook," Diana said. "You've been so kind to me since I arrived, and I thought maybe you could help me."

"Help you with cooking?" Keri asked. "Why, I'd be delighted! Let's start with what you can cook now."

"Pancakes," Diana said proudly.

"Pancakes. And?"

Diana shook her head. "No and. Just pancakes."

As they entered Keri's kitchen, Diana couldn't help but marvel at the organized space before her. Pots and pans hung neatly from hooks, and various utensils and spices lined the countertops. The aroma of freshly baked bread filled the air, making Diana's stomach rumble in anticipation.

"All right, let's begin with something simple," Keri said, rolling up her sleeves. "How about we start with bread? You're going to need bread every day."

"Sounds perfect," Diana replied, her eyes wide with wonder as Keri gathered the necessary ingredients.

She was determined to make cooking and baking a success, not only for Kevin but also for herself. It felt like a tangible way to prove her commitment to their marriage.

"All right, Diana," Keri began, her hands dusted with flour. "Making bread is an art, but once you get the hang of it, there's nothing quite like it."

Diana, still feeling a bit out of place in this new life, couldn't help but feel grateful for Keri's guidance. "I've never made bread before, so I appreciate your help, Keri."

Keri smiled warmly at Diana, her green eyes reflecting the determination she poured into every aspect of her life—from her work as a writer of mail-order bride romances to being a loving wife to Harry. "Don't worry, we'll take it step by step. Let's start with the basics."

As Keri explained the process, Diana found herself marveling at how skilled Keri was at not only writing but also at making the simplest tasks seem fun.

"First, we need to activate the yeast," Keri instructed, pouring warm water into a bowl. "Now, add a pinch of sugar and give it a good stir. You'll see it start to foam and bubble—that means the yeast is alive and ready to make the bread rise."

Diana followed her instructions, and within moments, the mixture came to life. She felt a thrill of accomplishment course through her, something she hadn't experienced in quite some time.

"Next, we'll add the flour," Keri continued, scooping a generous helping into the bowl. "Bread-making is as much about feel as it is about measurements. You want the dough to be soft and pliable but not too sticky."

Diana nodded, watching as Keri demonstrated the proper way to mix the ingredients with her hands. There was something almost meditative about the rhythmic motion of her hands folding and pressing the dough.

"Your turn," Keri encouraged, stepping back to give Diana room.

Emulating Keri's movements, Diana found herself lost in the process.

"Perfect!" Keri exclaimed, breaking Diana from her reverie. "Now we let it rise, and then we'll shape it into loaves."

As they waited for the dough to double in size, the two women shared stories and laughter, a bond forming between them. And when it was time, they rolled up their sleeves once more and set to work shaping the dough.

"Thank you, Keri," Diana said softly, her heart swelling with gratitude at the simple act of making bread together. "This means more to me than you know."

Keri smiled, reaching out to squeeze Diana's flour-dusted hand. "You're welcome, Diana. We all need a little help sometimes, and I'm just glad I can be here for you."

"Can you give me an easy receipt for supper tonight? I'll have bread of course, but if Kevin won't eat pancakes for every meal, he certainly won't do so with bread."

"Let's make supper together," Keri suggested. "I have more ham than I'll use for one meal."

"Thank you," Diana said, grinning.

"I'll show you how to bake a ham, and then we'll make some creamed potatoes to go with it."

"I'm sure that will be welcome after several meals in a row of pancakes."

Keri laughed. "He hasn't been complaining, so you're fine." She took a potato and carefully peeled it before slicing it into thin slices. And then another. Diana reached for a third potato, and imitated what Keri was doing.

"Perfect," Keri replied with a smile, her eyes crinkling at the corners. "You're doing great, Diana."

Diana couldn't help but smile back, feeling a swell of pride at the compliment. She focused on the task at hand, peeling several small potatoes as she mimicked Keri.

"Keri, do you think Kevin will like this?" she asked quietly, her eyes flicking toward the doorway as if expecting him to appear at any moment.

"Of course, he will," Keri reassured her. "He'll be so proud to see how hard you're working to learn something new."

A soft sigh of relief escaped Diana's lips, and she turned her attention back to the work she was doing.

An hour later, Keri said, "Okay, let's give it a taste," before handing Diana a spoon.

Diana hesitated for a moment, her heart pounding in anticipation. Would this dish be the perfect symbol of her dedication to their marriage? She dipped the spoon into the pot, brought it to her lips, and tasted the fruits of their labor.

"This isn't bad! Did I really make this myself?" Diana asked. "You didn't help with this pot, did you?"

Keri chuckled. "That's the spirit! Cooking is like any other skill—practice makes perfect. And trust me, Kevin will appreciate your efforts, even if they don't turn out perfectly every time."

"Would you be all right if I came over again tomorrow, and we cooked something different?"

Keri smiled, nodding. "Do that. After a couple of weeks, it'll be enough for me to just write the receipts down for you."

Feeling a newfound confidence, Diana stirred the pot with gusto, allowing herself to enjoy the process without fear of failure.

The soft clatter of cooking utensils and the warm, inviting aroma of ham filled the air as Diana confidently plated the meal. Her heart fluttered with anticipation, eager to impress her husband with her newfound culinary skills. Thank heavens Keri had been willing to teach her to cook.

"Diana, that smells amazing," Kevin's voice came from behind her, causing her heart to skip a beat. She hadn't realized he'd come up behind her.

"Thank you," she said, cheeks flushed with a mix of pride and nerves. "I spent the day with Keri, and we cooked together."

"You did all this?" he asked, more than a little surprised by all she had learned in just one day.

"Yes, well, with Keri's guidance, of course," she admitted modestly, her hands fidgeting with the edge of her apron. "I wanted to make a special meal."

"Diana, this looks incredible," Kevin said, his appreciation evident.

She beamed, feeling a swell of pride in her chest. "I'm still learning, but I'm determined to become a good wife and make our marriage work. And if that means spending a little extra time in the kitchen, then so be it."

"Your efforts are truly appreciated," he told her sincerely, his gaze meeting hers.

As they shared this tender moment, Diana couldn't help but feel hopeful for their future together. She may not know how to cook now, but she would learn. For Kevin. Good wives worked to keep their husbands happy.

"Shall we eat?" she asked, as she put the rest of the meal on the table.

"Absolutely," Kevin replied, happily taking his seat.

Diana held her breath as she watched Kevin take the first bite of the meal she had prepared. Her heart raced in anticipation, hoping that her newfound skills would please him.

"Diana, this is delicious," he said, savoring the flavors as they danced on his tongue.

"Really? You're not just saying that?" she asked, her eyes shining with hope.

"Of course not. I mean it," he replied, taking another bite and offering her a warm smile. "You've truly outdone yourself."

A wave of relief washed over Diana, followed by a rush of pride. She would keep going to Keri to learn as much as she could. Soon, she would be able to cook without having to run across the snow covered field to get daily lessons.

"Thank you, Kevin," she said softly, returning his smile.

Chapter Four

Diana stood in the kitchen of their newlywed home, her eyes trailing over the chipped and mismatched dishes stacked haphazardly in the cupboards. She sighed softly, running her fingers over a cracked plate, its once vibrant floral pattern now faded with age.

"Kevin, I think we should invest in some new dishes," Diana said, her voice gentle yet determined. "These are barely holding together."

"You know, you're right," he agreed, nodding thoughtfully. The corners of his mouth twitched into a warm smile that reached his eyes. "We can't keep using these old things forever."

"What if we buy some expensive, high-quality dishes? They will last longer and look nicer," she suggested tentatively. "There are some in the catalog that look really pretty to me, and they're from a quality company."

Kevin raised an eyebrow, clearly taken aback by her suggestion. "Are you sure? Those fancy sets can cost a small fortune." His voice held no judgment, only concern for their shared finances.

She nodded, firm in her decision. "I know, but I think it's worth it. We deserve something nice, don't you think?" She looked into his eyes, searching for understanding.

"All right," Kevin consented, his gaze softening. "If it's important to you, then let's do it. We'll have to save up for a few months to afford them, but if they'll last longer than the others, it'll be worth it in the end."

The scent of freshly brewed coffee filled the small kitchen, mingling with the warm light that streamed in through the window. Diana and Kevin sat at their cozy, wooden table, sipping from mismatched mugs as they continued the conversation about replacing their dishes.

"Diana, I understand you want something nice," Kevin began, his calloused hands gently cradling his favorite mug which had many chips. "But we should try to live within our means. I was looking in the catalog, and we just can't afford most of that stuff."

She hesitated, torn between her desire for beautiful things and her secret wealth. If only she could tell him the truth, share the burden of her inheritance. But would he still love her the same way?

"Perhaps you're right," she conceded. She tried to think of a compromise that wouldn't betray her secret. "We don't need the most expensive set, but maybe we can find something a little nicer than the basics?"

Kevin smiled, leaning back in his chair and running a hand through his tousled hair. "That sounds like a better plan." He shook his head. "It's a hard spot to be in. I want to give you the world, but I know we can't afford the world."

Her heart warmed at his words. "It'll be fun to find just the right set."

"Besides," Kevin added, his eyes twinkling with humor, "if we're going to be spending our hard-earned money on dishes, we might as well make sure they're something we both like."

"Agreed," Diana replied, reaching across the table to squeeze his hand. She knew deep down that it was not the dishes that mattered, but the life they were building together—one filled with love, trust, and just enough adventure to keep things interesting.

Diana shifted in her chair, her fingers tapping against the wooden table. The afternoon sun filtered through the curtains, casting a warm glow on the mismatched dishes that adorned their kitchen shelves. She could feel Kevin's gaze lingering on her, and she tried to put on a brave face. But the weight of her secret hung heavy on her heart.

"What's wrong?" Kevin asked, reaching out to touch her hand. His voice was gentle, laced with concern, and it struck a chord deep within her.

Diana looked into his earnest eyes, and she made a decision. "There's something I need to tell you. Something I've been hiding..."

"Diana, you can tell me anything," he assured her, giving her hand a reassuring squeeze.

"All right," she began, swallowing hard. "You know how we've been talking about living within our means? Well, the truth is...I have quite a lot of money saved up."

"Really?"

She knew she had kept this from him for far too long, but she couldn't bear the thought of him feeling betrayed by her deception. "Yes," she continued, her voice shaking slightly. "My parents left me a significant amount of money when they passed away. I didn't want anyone to know because... I wanted to be loved for who I am, not for my wealth." As she finished speaking, she forced herself to meet his gaze.

"Diana," Kevin whispered. "I will never be a wealthy man. You're going to learn to live within our means."

"Please don't be upset with me," she implored.

His thumb gently stroked her hand. "I can understand why you kept this from me, but it doesn't change how I feel about you. You're still the woman who came across the country to marry me and fed me pancakes more times than a man should have to eat them."

"Thank you," she whispered, feeling a weight lift off her chest as she leaned into his embrace. "I promise to be more open with you going forward." She grinned at him. "Let's find some dishes we both love for now."

"Deal," Kevin agreed, a warm smile lighting up his face.

Together, they continued to browse the selection of dishes, their hands occasionally brushing as they held each other's gaze. Each touch, every shared smile, was a testament to their commitment to building a life together based on love and trust - a partnership that would endure the test of time.

The crisp autumn air embraced Diana and Kevin as they stepped out of their cozy little home, the snow crunching beneath their feet.

"This will be our first real purchase together," Diana mused, her eyes dancing with anticipation. "I think I'd like something classic and timeless, but also with a touch of whimsy."

"Sounds good to me," Kevin agreed, his strong fingers intertwined with hers. Truthfully, he didn't care much about the dishes they bought. As long as they weren't too expensive.

"Do you remember that cute little shop we passed by last Sunday?" Diana asked, excitement bubbling within her. "I bet they'll have something unique. And today they'll be open."

"Of course, the one with the hand-painted sign?" Kevin replied, his eyes lighting up at the memory. "I think that's the perfect place to start."

They didn't talk a lot on their way to town, simply enjoying the extra time with one another since he had the day off.

As they stepped into the store, Diana's eyes scanned the eclectic displays. "Wow, there are so many options," Diana whispered, her fingertips grazing the smooth porcelain edges of various plates and bowls. "How will we ever choose?"

"Let's take our time," Kevin suggested, his gaze lingering on a particular set with delicate floral patterns. "We need to find something that speaks to both our hearts."

"Look at this one," Diana said, holding up a cream-colored plate adorned with intertwining vines and small, intricate flowers. "There's something so enchanting about it."

"You took the words right out of my mouth," Kevin replied, his smile reflecting her own. "I can imagine us sharing meals on these plates for years to come."

"Me too," she whispered.

"Let's get these," Kevin said, his voice full of warmth and affection.

Diana clutched a wad of cash in her hand, discreetly tucked beneath the billfold to ensure Kevin wouldn't suspect anything. Her heart raced as she approached the counter, aware that this small act might determine the course of their future together.

"Can I help you with anything else?" the store clerk asked, glancing at Diana and Kevin as they stood side by side.

"No, thank you," Diana replied, offering a polite smile. "We'd just like to purchase these dishes, please."

"All right then." The clerk expertly rang up the set, and wrapped each piece in brown paper before placing them into a sturdy crate.

"Your total comes to thirty-seven dollars, and fourteen cents," the clerk announced, snapping Diana back to the present moment. She hesitated for only a second before handing over the wad of bills, her heart skipping a beat when Kevin glanced her way.

"Are you sure you want to spend this much?" he asked, his eyes searching hers for any sign of doubt or hesitation.

"Yes, absolutely. These are the dishes we liked best."

"True," Kevin conceded, returning her smile with a gentle one of his own. "I just don't want you to feel like you're spending too much."

"I don't at all!"

As the clerk handed Diana her change and the box of dishes, she felt a surge of excitement. As she left the store, she realized it may have been better to give Kevin the money before going inside so he could pay. Some men were odd about that.

"Let's go home and make our first meal together on these dishes," Diana suggested as Kevin took the box from her to put it in the back of the wagon.

She was thrilled he'd agreed to use her money, and she thought maybe she could get him to use it a little more, so their life could be just a bit more comfortable.

THE SUN DIPPED LOW on the horizon as Diana stood at the window, gazing out at the warm orange hues that painted the sky. She smiled to herself, feeling a flutter of excitement in her chest. Tonight, she and Kevin were having supper with their friends Harry and Keri at the Whites' ranch. It had been a while since all four of them had been together, and Diana was eager for both the company and the opportunity to learn from their experiences.

"Are you ready?" Kevin's voice sounded from behind her, pulling her from her thoughts.

Diana turned to see him standing in the doorway, looking as handsome as ever. "Yes, I am," she replied with a smile. "I just can't help but feel a little nervous."

Kevin walked over and took her hand, giving it a reassuring squeeze. "Don't worry."

"Thank you," she said softly, leaning against him briefly before stepping back. "All right, let's go!"

They walked the short distance across the ranch and she happily knocked on Keri's door.

Diana and Kevin made their way to the front door, where they were greeted with open arms by Harry and Keri.

"Welcome!" Keri exclaimed, her eyes twinkling with delight. "We've missed you both so much!"

"I was here yesterday," Diana said with a laugh. "And I know that Kevin and Harry worked together today. Are you *sure* you missed us?"

Keri shrugged. "Sometimes it's exciting to see other people!"

Diana laughed. "I agree. There were too many people back east, and here there are way too few. Thank you for having us," Diana said.

As they settled in for their evening of laughter, conversation, and good food, Diana couldn't help but feel grateful for the friends who had become more like family.

The scent of roasted chicken mingled with the enticing aroma of fresh-baked bread, awakening her senses and drawing her into the present moment.

"How's your book coming?" Diana asked, eager to read what the other woman wrote.

"Almost done," Keri said. "A few more mornings of waking up at two to get words in, and I'll be all done. I'm so thankful for the typewriter Harry bought me. It's making so much difference in the amount of time it takes me to finish a book."

There's a continuity issue with this. Harry bought her a typewriter after their baby was born. She was carrying her baby when the typewriter and her first books arrived. You make this seem like she's published several books but inly been married a few months. This is the only place you mention the typewriter

Laughter bubbled around the table, punctuating the comfortable conversation that flowed between them. As the evening progressed, Diana gathered the courage to broach a topic that had been weighing on her mind. "Harry, Keri," she began, taking a bite of her chicken, "Kevin and I were wondering if you might have some advice for us, in regards to navigating married life and building a strong partnership."

"Of course!" Keri said enthusiastically. "Navigating marriage is an ongoing journey, but one we'd be more than happy to share our insights on. Of course, we just got married in June, so we don't have a ton of experience to draw on."

"Communication is key," Harry started, his voice steady and reassuring. "Always be open and honest with each other, even when it's difficult. And remember that listening is just as important as speaking."

Diana nodded, soaking in his words like a sponge.

"Also, give each other space to grow," Keri added, her own experiences shining through in her eyes. "Supporting one another's dreams and aspirations is essential for a strong partnership."

"Thank you both so much," Kevin said sincerely.

"Always happy to help," Harry replied, raising his glass of milk in a toast. "To love, friendship, and the adventures that lie ahead."

As they clinked glasses and sipped milk, Diana felt a renewed sense of confidence in her marriage.

"You know," Keri began, stirring her tea thoughtfully, "the only real difficulty Harry and I faced in the beginning was my need to write at unusual hours."

"Unusual hours?" Diana asked.

Keri chuckled, her eyes alight with amusement. "Yes, you see, I get ideas at the oddest times, often in the dead of night. I'd stay up writing while Harry slept, and he couldn't quite understand why I wanted to write instead of sleeping when he did."

"Ah, I see," Kevin chimed in.

Harry exchanged a knowing smile with his wife. "Well, it took some time for us to adjust, but eventually, we realized that giving each other space to pursue our own interests and passions was crucial for our relationship to thrive."

"Exactly," Keri added. "We learned that patience was essential in allowing both of us to grow and adapt to our new lives together."

"Building a successful marriage requires understanding and acceptance," Harry continued. "It's important to remember that every relationship is unique, and what works for one couple might not work for another."

"Indeed," Keri agreed.

Chapter Six

"Kevin, are you awake?" Diana whispered early one morning, turning to see him already sitting up, a smile gracing his rugged features.

"Morning," he replied, his voice still rough from sleep. "I've been up for a while, couldn't wait to get out there and show you this beautiful land." His eyes sparkled with anticipation.

Diana smiled, feeling her heart swell with affection for this man who had become her husband just four weeks prior. They had yet to experience the true depths of love, but she knew that moments like these would forge the bond between them.

"Let's not waste any more time then," she said, quickly getting up. They busied themselves in the kitchen, preparing a picnic lunch of fried chicken, mashed potatoes, green beans, and creamy gravy—a meal fit for royalty.

"Did you make all this yourself?" Kevin asked, impressed by her culinary skills. Diana chuckled softly.

"Actually, Keri taught me how to make it. I wanted to surprise you and show my appreciation for everything you've done for me."

"Just having you here is enough," he replied, his voice filled with warmth and sincerity. He reached out and pulled her into his arms.

Once the food was packed neatly into baskets, they ventured out to the stable where Kevin's sleigh waited. The horses greeted them with soft whinnies, anticipating the day's adventure. Diana's eyes widened in surprise when she saw the sleigh, having never seen one so ornate before.

"Is this for us?" she asked, and Kevin nodded proudly.

"Harry and Keri insisted," he explained. "They wanted to make sure we had a memorable day." The thoughtfulness of the gesture warmed

Diana's heart, and she couldn't help but feel grateful for the support they'd received from his employers.

With everything loaded into the back of the sleigh, they set off on their journey, the horses' hooves crunching in the snow as they moved through the crisp morning air. As they traveled, Diana couldn't help but marvel at the vast open spaces that stretched out before them, the majestic mountains in the distance calling her name.

"Kevin, thank you for bringing me here," she whispered, her hand finding his as they sat side by side on the sleigh. "I never knew such beauty existed."

"It's my pleasure," he replied, giving her hand a gentle squeeze. "And I promise you, there's so much more to see."

Diana gazed upon the Wyoming countryside, the picturesque landscape a stark contrast to her life in Massachusetts. The rolling plains seemed to stretch on forever, and far off in the distance, the majestic mountains loomed like silent guardians. She found herself captivated by their beauty, a sense of wonder and awe filling her heart.

"Kevin, I can't believe how different this is from back home," she said, her words carried away by the gentle breeze. "It's as if I've stepped into another world."

He glanced at her with a warm smile, his eyes filled with pride for the land he loved. "Wyoming has a way of doing that to people. It's a place that'll change your life if you let it. Over there looks perfect!" Kevin exclaimed, pointing to a secluded spot beside a crystal-clear mountain stream. He guided the sleigh to a stop, and Diana eagerly hopped down, her boots crunching on the snow-covered ground.

"Wow, this is amazing," she breathed, her eyes wide with delight as she took in the idyllic scene before them. "I can't believe we're actually here."

"Neither can I," Kevin admitted, his voice soft and tender as he looked at her. "But I'm glad we are."

They unpacked their picnic lunch, spreading out a blanket on the snow-dusted ground near the babbling stream. "Maybe we should have picked a warmer day for this," she said with a laugh. "Is it crazy to have picnics in the snow?"

He looked at her, his eyes filled with emotion. "If it's crazy, then I'm glad we're not sane," he said, the laughter in his eyes comforting her in a way nothing else in life really had.

Diana looked at the spread of food she had prepared, feeling a mixture of pride and trepidation. The sun glinted off the crystal-clear stream beside them, casting dancing reflections on the snow around their picnic blanket. She watched Kevin take a bite of her fried chicken, her breath catching in anticipation.

"Wow, Diana," he said, his eyes widening in genuine surprise. "This is amazing! I wouldn't have believed it if I hadn't tasted it myself." He took another bite, savoring the flavors before swallowing. "And these mashed potatoes, they're so creamy and smooth."

"Thank you," she replied, feeling a warm blush creep up her cheeks as she focused on cutting into her own piece of chicken. "I'm glad you like it. I was worried I might mess it up somehow."

"Are you kidding me?" Kevin chuckled, reaching across to squeeze her hand lightly. "You have a real gift for cooking. And these green beans with creamy gravy? Delicious. I think I'm going to have to start calling you 'the culinary queen.'"

Diana laughed, her heart swelling with happiness. It felt so good to be appreciated for something other than her money or social status. "Well, I do enjoy cooking," she admitted. "It's a wonderful way for me to relax and express myself."

"Then I consider myself a very lucky man," he said, his gaze tender and warm as he looked at her. "Not only are you beautiful and kind, but also incredibly talented."

Diana felt the heat of his words deep within her chest. In that moment, she realized that she truly desired Kevin's love and affection, more than anything else in the world.

"Kevin," she whispered, the sound of his name on her lips feeling like a secret prayer. "I truly enjoy being with you, and I hope...I hope that we can find happiness together."

His eyes softened, and he reached for her hand once more, intertwining their fingers. "From the moment I laid eyes on you, I knew there was something special about you. You've already brought so much happiness into my life, and I promise you, I will do everything in my power to make you happy too."

DIANA SIGHED, HER FINGERS tracing the edge of an envelope she had just received. The letter inside bore disturbing news, indeed.

"Kevin?" she called out, her voice wavering ever so slightly. "Could you come here for a moment?"

"Of course," Kevin replied, his footsteps echoing down the hallway before he appeared in the doorway. His strong frame leaned against the doorframe, curiosity etched on his handsome face as he took in the sight of his wife, clutching a letter. "What's wrong, Diana?"

"My cousin George sent a letter." She swallowed hard, her eyes meeting Kevin's concerned gaze. "He claims that my inheritance should have gone to him."

"George?" Kevin frowned, stepping into the room and gently taking the letter from her trembling hands. As he read through it, his brow furrowed even deeper. "But why now? Your parents have been gone for months."

"Exactly," Diana murmured, her heart sinking with each word she recalled from the letter. Her inheritance wasn't something she wanted to think about, but it seemed that George had other plans. "He says that he was their closest male relative at the time of their demise, therefore he has a right to what they left behind."

"Let me see if I understand this correctly," Kevin said slowly, folding the letter and handing it back to her. "He thinks he can waltz in and claim your inheritance just because he's related to you?"

Diana nodded, biting her lower lip in apprehension. "That's what he's saying. And, honestly, I don't know how to handle this."

"Look," Kevin said, his voice firm and reassuring as he placed a hand on her shoulder. "You are the rightful heir to your parents' estate. Not George. We will fight this, Diana."

"Thank you." Diana leaned into his embrace, her breath hitching as she allowed herself a moment of vulnerability.

"Have you considered reaching out to your lawyer?" Kevin asked, his voice breaking through her reverie. He leaned against the door frame, his brow furrowed with concern.

Diana turned to face him, her eyes glistening with unshed tears. "I think I'll have to," she admitted, her voice barely above a whisper. "I just never expected any of my family to try and take away what my parents left me."

"George's actions are selfish and unjust," Kevin said firmly, striding across the room to stand beside her. "But we won't let him succeed. You deserve every bit of your inheritance, Diana."

Taking a deep breath, Diana nodded. "You're right. I need to protect what's mine—what my parents wanted for me." As she spoke, her resolve strengthened. She wouldn't let George's greed affect her.

"Then it's decided," Kevin said, his hand finding hers and giving it a reassuring squeeze. "We'll contact your lawyer and prepare for whatever comes next."

Together, they sat down at the small desk in their bedroom, and Diana penned a letter to her lawyer, explaining the situation and requesting his assistance. The response came swiftly, and within days, they were preparing to leave for Cheyenne, where the trial would take place.

As they packed their bags for the journey, Diana couldn't help but feel a sense of trepidation. But each time her thoughts threatened to spiral into fear, she reminded herself of Kevin's unwavering support.

When they arrived in Cheyenne, their lawyer met them at the hotel where they would be staying for the next couple of nights. With his guidance, they discussed strategy and prepared for the upcoming court battle.

Throughout it all, Diana felt comforted by the fact that she wasn't alone. She had Kevin by her side, and together, they would stand strong against George's claims.

Diana nervously adjusted the collar of her dress as she glanced around the austere courthouse. The polished wooden benches loomed before her, and the air was thick with anticipation. She felt Kevin's warm hand envelop hers, offering reassurance.

"Everything will be all right," he murmured, his deep voice soothing her jangled nerves.

As they entered the courtroom, Diana's heart raced, and the knot in her stomach tightened. She knew that this trial would be an uphill battle, but with Kevin by her side, she felt more capable of facing it.

"Order in the court!" the bailiff bellowed, silencing the murmurs of onlookers.

George, a portly man with a smug expression, stood to address the judge. "Your Honor, I was the closest male relative to Diana's parents when they passed away. It's only fair that I inherit their wealth as per tradition."

Diana clenched her jaw, her anger rising at his audacity. She could not let him win. Her mind raced, searching for a way to prove her worthiness of the inheritance. She thought back to her late-night conversations with Kevin, when they had shared their dreams of using her inheritance for him to go to college or to buy a ranch of their own.

"Your Honor," she interrupted, her voice steady and determined, "I understand that my cousin believes he is entitled to my parents' money, but I can assure you, I have every intention of honoring their memory by using their fortune wisely and responsibly."

"Miss Diana," the judge warned, "please let your lawyer speak on your behalf."

"Apologies, Your Honor," she whispered, her cheeks flushing with embarrassment.

As Mr. Thompson stood to defend her claim, she glanced over at Kevin.

The sound of the gavel striking the wooden block echoed through the courtroom, sending a shiver down Diana's spine. She clutched her hands tightly in her lap, her knuckles white from the pressure. Her gaze flickered between the judge and George, trying to read their expressions as she held her breath.

"Mr. Thompson," the judge began, addressing Diana's lawyer, "you have presented a compelling case on behalf of your client. I find it difficult to accept Mr. George's argument that he is entitled to the inheritance based solely on his being the closest male relative."

Diana's heart swelled with hope, her fingers trembling slightly as she allowed herself to believe that maybe, just maybe, she could win this battle.

"Furthermore," the judge continued, "it has been made clear that Miss Diana has every intention of using her inheritance for the betterment of herself, her family, and her community."

"Based on the evidence presented, I hereby rule in favor of Miss Diana and order that the inheritance in question be granted to her," the judge declared, meeting George's stunned expression with an unyielding gaze. "Mr. George, I suggest you go back home and make peace with this decision. This court will not entertain any further attempts to challenge Miss Diana's rightful claim."

"Thank you, Your Honor," Diana exhaled, relief washing over her like a warm wave.

"Congratulations, Diana," Kevin whispered, squeezing her hand gently as they stood to leave the courtroom.

George glared at them as they left to return home, and Diana simply breezed by him. Why the man thought her money should be his was beyond her in the first place.

Chapter Seven

Thankfully, George slunk back to Massachusetts, and they didn't have to deal with him again. As the months passed, Diana learned more and more about being a wife in the west. There were so many things she'd never learned that she quickly became adept at under Keri's tutelage.

Diana stood by the window, her gaze fixed on the snow-covered landscape of the ranch. She watched with a barely contained excitement as the morning sun began to melt the snow, revealing patches of green grass beneath.

"Look, Keri," she said, gesturing to the scene outside. "The snow is melting."

Keri, Harry's wife, and creator of the mail-order bride romances, smiled warmly at Diana. "Yes, it happens every year!"

As Diana continued to watch the transformation outside, an idea that had been slowly forming in her mind began to solidify. She knew that Kevin deserved more than just being a ranch foreman. He had shown exceptional care and kindness to both people and animals during their time together, qualities that would make him an excellent doctor.

"Keri," she began hesitantly, "I've been thinking about something lately. You know how skilled Kevin is when it comes to taking care of the ranch and all the animals?"

"Of course," Keri replied. "He's got a real gift for it."

"Exactly. That's what I've been thinking too. And it made me wonder... What if he could use those skills to help even more people?" Diana paused, her heart pounding in her chest as she gathered the courage to voice her thoughts. "What if he went to medical school and became a doctor?"

Keri's eyes widened at the suggestion, and she studied Diana's face for a moment before responding. "That's an interesting idea. But medical school is expensive, and it would mean leaving the ranch. I'd lose you and Harry would lose Kevin!"

"I know," Diana admitted, her voice barely above a whisper. "But I believe in him, Keri. And I think he could make a real difference in this world as a doctor." Her eyes welled up with unshed tears, but she wiped them away quickly. She didn't want to be seen as weak or overly emotional; she wanted to show that she was strong and capable of supporting Kevin in any endeavor.

Keri reached out and squeezed Diana's hand. "It's clear how much you care about him. I'll talk to Harry, and we'll see what we can do to help make this dream a reality for Kevin."

"Thank you," Diana whispered, her heart swelling with love and gratitude for her new family. As she watched the snow continue to melt outside the window, the image of Kevin as a doctor filled her mind, and she couldn't help but smile at the thought of the bright future they could share together.

Diana watched as Kevin guided his horse across the yard, his muscular frame silhouetted against the setting sun. The last remnants of winter ice clung stubbornly to the earth, but the first signs of spring were evident in the buds on the trees and the occasional chirping of a brave bird. She knew that with the changing seasons came new growth and fresh beginnings, and she felt it was time for change in their own lives as well.

"Kevin," she called out as he approached the porch where she stood, her voice soft yet determined. He looked up, his deep blue eyes meeting hers, a question in them. "I have something I want to discuss with you."

"Sure thing," he replied, dismounting and tying the reins to the hitching post. He followed her inside the cozy ranch house, an eager curiosity in his stride.

Once they were settled on the worn sofa, Diana took a deep breath and gathered her thoughts. She could feel her heart pounding in her chest, but she refused to let her nerves get the better of her. This was too important.

"Kevin," she began, her hands clenched together in her lap. "I've been thinking about our future. You're so incredibly talented and dedicated in everything you do here on the ranch, but I believe you have the potential to do even more."

"More?" he asked, his brow furrowing as he tried to decipher her meaning. "Do you have a problem with me being a ranch foreman?"

"Of course not! I care about you no matter what you do for a living. But you mentioned something to me once that I can't get out of my head." She took a deep breath. "Medical school," she blurted out, unable to contain her excitement any longer. "You could become a doctor and make such a difference in this world."

She held her breath as she gauged his reaction. He stared at her for a moment, his eyes searching hers for understanding. Then, slowly, he leaned back against the cushions, his gaze drifting to the window as he considered her words.

"Medical school is expensive," he said finally, his voice betraying a hint of uncertainty. "And it would mean leaving the ranch."

"My inheritance is more than enough to send you to school, and even help you start your practice when you're done. I would hope we could come back to this area, but that would be up to you. You wouldn't have to work except your studying."

"But I'm so much older than most students would be."

"I know," she replied, her fingers absently tracing patterns on the fabric of her skirt. "But I believe in you, Kevin. And I think we can make this work. Now, I've done my research, and I've found that the nearest medical school would be at the University of Colorado in Aurora."

He was silent for a moment, his eyes still fixed on the window as if seeking answers in the fading light. Then, with a sigh, he turned back to her and offered a small, tentative smile.

"Thank you for believing in me, Diana," he said softly. "I'll give it some thought."

Over the next few days, Diana watched as Kevin went about his usual routine, his mind clearly preoccupied with the decision before him. She knew how much he loved the ranch, but she also saw the spark of curiosity that ignited every time they discussed the possibility of a new career in medicine.

As calving season began, Diana found herself drawn to the barn to watch Kevin at work. He moved with a gentle confidence among the cows and their newborns, his hands sure and steady as he tended to their needs. In those quiet moments, she could already envision him as a doctor, his passion and skill improving the lives of countless patients.

"Kevin," she whispered one evening as they lay tangled together beneath the soft blankets, their bodies still warm from their lovemaking. "Whatever you decide, I just want you to know that I will support you, every step of the way."

He pulled her closer, pressing a tender kiss to her forehead. "I know," he murmured. "That means more to me than you could ever know."

As they drifted off to sleep, Diana felt a sense of peace settle over her. Whatever decision he made, she would be proud of her wonderful husband.

Diana stood in the kitchen, her hands coated in flour as she and Keri worked side by side to prepare for the upcoming round up. The smell of fresh bread filled the air, mingling with the scent of simmering beef stew that bubbled on the stove. Sunlight streamed through the window, casting a warm golden glow over the room. Diana couldn't help but smile as she thought about the party they were planning—a celebration for the successful round up, and a thank you to all the people who went out of their way to help with the castration of the young steers.

Diana nodded, her fingers working deftly as she formed the dough into loaves. She'd come a very long way in her cooking skills in just a few short months.

"Thank you, Keri," Diana said sincerely, placing the loaves on a baking sheet.

"For what?" Keri asked, turning back to the stew.

"For helping me so much in learning how to be a good wife. I don't know what I would have done without you."

Keri smiled. "I'm very happy to help. Now, let's get back to work. We have a party to plan!"

As they continued cooking, Diana's thoughts drifted to Kevin and the future that lay before them.

THE SUN WAS HIGH IN the sky as Diana and Keri drove down the dusty road toward town. The warm breeze carried the scent of wildflowers, and Diana couldn't help but feel a sense of excitement as she chatted with her new friend. Now that round up was over, there was time for other things, and this trip to town was a much-needed change of pace.

"Thank you for agreeing to come with me," Diana said, smiling at Keri. "I'm not quite used to navigating around here yet."

"Of course," Keri replied, her eyes crinkling at the corners as she smiled back. "I know how stir-crazy it can get out there on the ranch. Besides, I could use some company myself."

As they entered the town, Diana marveled at the quaint storefronts and friendly faces that greeted them. It wasn't long before they found themselves in a cozy general store, where Diana eagerly began browsing the shelves. Her eyes sparkled as she picked up various items—soap, candles, and doilies—envisioning how they would look in her home.

"Keri, what do you think of these?" Diana asked, holding up a pair of shiny black shoes. She turned them over in her hands, admiring the craftsmanship. "I've been wearing my old boots for so long now."

"Those are lovely, Diana," Keri said, nodding approvingly. "Why don't you try them on?"

Diana slipped off her worn boots and slid her feet into the new shoes. They fit perfectly, hugging her feet like a second skin. She took a few steps, reveling in the comfortable support they provided. "I think I'll take them," she decided, beaming.

"Excellent choice," Keri agreed, giving her an encouraging pat on the shoulder.

Next, Diana's gaze fell upon a rack of pre-made dresses. She rifled through them, searching for something that would suit her taste and the practical needs of life on the ranch. After a moment, she pulled out two lovely options—one a soft blue, the other a warm shade of red.

"Keri, which one should I choose?" Diana asked, holding the dresses up against her body in turn.

"I like the blue," Keri said, smiling.

Diana nodded, suddenly feeling very grown-up and independent as she looked at both and decided to buy two dresses. The thought of Kevin's reaction when he saw her in them sent a thrill down her spine.

As they continued browsing, Diana came across a beautiful set of pots and pans. The smooth metal surfaces gleamed under the store's light, promising a new world of culinary possibilities. "These would be perfect for our kitchen," she mused, running her fingers over the handles. "I've been making do with some old, rusty cookware we found in the cabin."

"New pots and pans can make such a difference," Keri agreed, admiring the set alongside Diana. "I remember when Harry got me a new set after we were first married. I felt like a real chef. But you may need to put back the shoes or dresses if you're getting those."

Diana frowned for a moment, but decided to buy them all anyway. Why not?

With her arms laden with her purchases, Diana couldn't shake the feeling that this was more than just a shopping trip. It was a declaration of her commitment to her new life with Kevin.

They entered the next store, its wooden sign creaking in the breeze.

"Goodness, you've spent quite a bit today, Diana," Keri remarked, her eyes widening at the ever-growing pile of purchases. "I hope Kevin won't be too upset."

Diana hesitated for a moment and then smiled. "He'll understand. We're starting our life together, after all. Besides, I have my own money to spend."

As they walked through the aisles, Diana's gaze fell upon an array of colorful packets, neatly organized in a large wooden display. A sense of excitement bubbled up inside her as she realized what they were: seeds for fruits, vegetables, and flowers.

"Look, Keri!" Diana exclaimed, picking up a packet of tomato seeds. "I'm so excited to plant my own garden! Imagine how proud Kevin will be when he sees the fruits of my labor. And we won't need to buy produce from the market anymore."

Keri nodded in agreement, impressed by Diana's enthusiasm. "I usually plant a garden as well. It's always nice to have fresh fruits and vegetables right outside your door."

Diana's excitement grew as she browsed the selection, adding packets of cucumber, carrot, and lettuce seeds to her basket. But it wasn't just the practical plants that caught her eye; she was also drawn to the delicate flowers that could bring beauty and color to their little cabin.

"Keri, look at these lovely flower seeds," Diana said, holding up packets of marigolds, lavender, and roses. "Wouldn't these be perfect for a small flower bed by our front porch?"

"Those are beautiful, but don't forget to consider the cost," Keri cautioned, her eyebrows knitting together with concern. "Flowers are lovely, but they're not essential."

"Perhaps not," Diana admitted, her eyes shining with determination. "But they'll make our home more inviting and cheerful. A little bit of beauty in the midst of all the hard work we have ahead of us can't hurt, right?"

Keri hesitated before giving a small smile. "You're right, Diana. Just remember to be mindful of your spending."

Diana nodded, her heart swelling with love and appreciation for her friend's concern. Though she had been fortunate enough to inherit a sizable fortune, she knew that Keri was only looking out for her best interests.

"Thank you, Keri," Diana murmured. "I promise I'll be careful."

Keri and Diana drove back to the ranch, the horses' hooves kicking up dust in rhythmic harmony. The scent of wildflowers carried on the breeze, and Diana closed her eyes for a moment, allowing herself to be enveloped by the beauty of the landscape.

"Are you sure you didn't go overboard with your shopping today?" Keri asked gently, breaking the companionable silence. Her gaze flickered toward the bags in the back of the wagon.

Diana opened her eyes and sighed, feeling the weight of her friend's concern. "I know it seems like a lot, but I promise I was careful." She hesitated, her fingers playing with the edge of one of the bags. "Besides, we needed those things for the cabin, and I wanted to make our home more welcoming."

"Of course," Keri replied, her tone softening. "But you need to remember that life out here is different than what you're used to back East. We have to live within our means, and sometimes that means making sacrifices."

Diana nodded, understanding Keri's intention but still feeling the sting of her words. She knew Keri was unaware of the fortune she had inherited, and without Kevin's permission, Diana wasn't willing to confide in her friend. Instead, she tried to focus on the positives of their conversation.

"Thank you for looking out for me, Keri," Diana said, offering her friend a small smile. "I'm still adjusting to this new way of life, but I'll try my best to be more mindful of our expenses."

"Good, I just want you to be prepared for the challenges ahead," Keri responded, returning the smile. "And I'm here to help you every step of the way."

Diana's heart swelled with gratitude, knowing she could rely on Keri's support. As they continued their ride, Diana allowed her thoughts to drift back to her shopping spree and the future that awaited them on the ranch. She imagined the fruits and vegetables growing in their garden, providing sustenance for their family, and the vibrant flowers adding a touch of beauty to the rugged landscape.

"Life here may be different," she thought to herself, "but it's the life I've chosen with Kevin. And together, we'll make it work."

The sun dipped lower in the sky, casting long shadows across the path as they drew closer to home. And as they crested the final hill, Diana caught sight of their cabin, its modest structure now holding the promise of love and dreams fulfilled.

The sun was setting as Diana and Keri arrived home. The sight of Kevin waiting on the porch to welcome them back sent a mixture of excitement and trepidation through Diana's veins.

"Hey there, ladies," Kevin greeted them with a smile that didn't quite reach his eyes. "Did you have a good time in town?"

"Of course! We found everything we needed," Keri replied cheerfully, setting the brake on the wagon and beginning to unload their bags. As she began carrying the items inside, she cast a sidelong glance at Diana, knowing full well what lay ahead for her friend.

"Let me help you with that," Kevin offered, reaching for one of the bags. As he lifted it, his brow furrowed, and he looked between the bag and Diana. "What in the world did you buy, Diana? This is heavy."

Diana flushed, suddenly feeling self-conscious about her purchases. "Just some necessities," she murmured, trying to sound nonchalant. "New shoes, dresses, pots and pans... and seeds for our garden."

"Seeds?" Kevin's voice held a note of exasperation. "How many seeds does one person need?"

"Kevin, I thought it would be nice to grow some fruits, vegetables, and flowers to brighten up our home," she explained defensively.

"Really now?" He set the bags down and turned to face her fully, concern etching lines into his handsome face. "Diana, we talked about this. We're saving for medical school, remember? We can't afford to splurge on unnecessary things."

"Unnecessary?" She bristled, her heart pounding in her chest. "I'm trying to make our home more beautiful and provide food for us. How is that unnecessary?"

"Flowers are an extravagance we can't afford," he argued, his voice rising in frustration. "And we don't need a dozen different types of fruits and vegetables!"

"Kevin, I'm doing the best I can to adjust to this new life," Diana protested, tears prickling at the corners of her eyes. "I thought you would appreciate my efforts."

"Your efforts are appreciated, but they need to be practical," he shot back, rubbing a hand over his face. "We have to live within our means, Diana. If we keep spending like this, we'll never be able to afford medical school. Our future depends on it."

As she looked into Kevin's worried eyes, she wanted nothing more than to reveal just how much money she had. But she had made a promise to herself— and to Kevin—that their love would not be built on money.

"All right, Kevin," she conceded, her voice thick with unshed tears. "I promise I'll be more careful with our expenses from now on."

"Thank you," he said softly, reaching out to wrap her in a comforting embrace. "I just want what's best for us."

Diana stood in the doorway of their shared bedroom, watching Kevin as he methodically packed his medical books into a worn leather satchel. The afternoon sun cast a warm glow on his face, highlighting the lines of worry etched around his eyes. A pang of guilt twisted her stomach, knowing she was the cause of that worry.

"Kevin," she began hesitantly, wringing her hands together. "There's something I need to tell you."

He paused in his packing and looked up at her with a questioning gaze. "What is it?"

She took a deep breath, her heart racing in her chest. "I haven't been completely honest with you about my financial situation."

His brow furrowed, clearly confused by her confession. "What do you mean?"

"Well, you know my parents left me an inheritance," she explained, her voice barely above a whisper. It felt like a weight was being lifted from her shoulders as she finally confessed what she had been hiding for so long. "Much larger than I've let on."

"Larger?" Kevin echoed, setting the satchel down on the bed and taking a step toward her. "How large are we talking here, Diana?"

"Over a million dollars," she admitted, feeling a mix of shame and relief as the truth tumbled out.

Kevin's eyes widened, shock overtaking his features. For a moment, he seemed lost for words, simply staring at her as if he couldn't quite comprehend what she had just told him.

"A million dollars?" he finally managed to choke out. "You have over a million dollars at your disposal?"

She nodded, biting her lip. "Yes. I'm sorry I didn't tell you sooner. I wanted you to love me for who I am, not for the money I brought with me."

As the reality of her confession settled in, Kevin sank onto the edge of the bed, looking utterly overwhelmed. He ran a hand through his hair, his expression a mixture of disbelief and concern.

"God, Diana," he murmured, shaking his head. "I knew your family was well off, but I never imagined you had that much money."

She took a tentative step closer to him, reaching out to touch his arm. "It doesn't change how I feel about you, Kevin. I love you for who you are, not what you can provide for me."

He looked up at her, his blue eyes filled with insecurity. "But how can I ever be enough for you? How can I possibly give you the life you deserve when you have so much more than I could ever offer?"

"Kevin, listen to me," she implored, gripping his arm tightly. "You are enough. More than enough. The life we're building together means more to me than any amount of money ever could. Promise me you believe that."

He hesitated for a moment, and then slowly nodded. "I promise," he said, his voice thick with emotion.

With that, they pulled each other close, sealing their newfound trust with a tender embrace. Together, they would face whatever challenges life had in store for them—as equals, bound by love rather than financial gains.

Chapter Eight

The train's whistle pierced the air as it pulled into the station, a cloud of steam billowing around it like a dense fog. Diana clutched her small traveling bag close to her chest, her heart thudding with anticipation. Beside her, Kevin stood tall and sturdy, his shoulders squared as he prepared for their journey.

"Are you ready?" Kevin asked, his voice gentle but firm as he looked at Diana with reassurance in his dark eyes.

Diana took a deep breath, her hands trembling ever so slightly from excitement. "I think so," she replied, offering him a brave smile.

Together, they boarded the train to Colorado, the prospect of visiting the medical school in Aurora looming before them like a beacon of hope. As they settled into their sleeping car, Diana couldn't help but watch Kevin's strong profile, admiring the determination etched on his handsome face. She knew how much this opportunity meant to him, and she was determined to support him every step of the way.

"Are you excited that you can finally achieve your goal of becoming a doctor?" Diana ventured.

Kevin's eyes softened as he glanced at her. "Ever since I was a boy, I've been drawn to helping people," he said, his voice filled with passion. "I reckon it's just a part of who I am."

Diana felt a warmth spread through her chest at his words. She yearned to see him succeed, to witness him achieve his dreams. The closer they drew to Aurora, the more excited she became for him and his future. For their shared future.

Upon their arrival, they made their way to the medical school, surrounded by the bustling cityscape. The campus loomed ahead, its buildings imposing yet inviting, a testament to the knowledge housed within.

As they walked through the halls, Diana couldn't help but feel a sense of awe. "Just think, you could be studying here in just a matter of months," she whispered, her voice hushed with reverence.

Kevin's eyes sparkled with ambition, his gaze sweeping over the surroundings as he took it all in. Finally, they reached the admissions office, where Kevin filled out the necessary paperwork to apply for the fall semester.

"Are you sure this is what you want?" Diana asked, her hand resting on his forearm as he signed his name on the application form.

"More than anything," he replied, his voice steady with determination. "But I wouldn't be here without your support, Diana."

As they turned to leave the office, the weight of Kevin's future hanging in the balance, Diana felt an undeniable sense of optimism. Whatever the outcome, whether he was accepted into medical school or not, she vowed to stand by him, to be his partner in every sense of the word. And as they stepped back out into the world, hand in hand, she couldn't help but hope that love might eventually blossom between them, too.

They stayed in a hotel in Denver that evening, and even had supper in the dining room there at the hotel. As they walked into the room, the chandeliers seemed to drip opulence. So much money wasted on a pricy room and expensive dishes. Money that could have been spent for medicines and proper medical treatment.

It was amazing to Kevin to see how well she fit into the wealth around them, and he felt that she was far away from him. "How am I supposed to know which fork to use?" he asked, making a face.

"Just follow what I do," she said softly. "You usually start from the outside and go in."

Kevin shook his head. "I think I'm going to need lessons if we're going to eat in places like this often."

Diana laughed. "As far as I'm concerned, you can dip your knife in mashed potatoes, and use it to eat peas off the knife. Truly, I don't care. But I do enjoy good food, and that's what we'll be served here."

Kevin smiled, but stared down at the silverware, wishing he knew the proper utensil to use for each part of the meal. He felt so out of place in the fancy restaurant, and he knew that his good Sunday suit was lacking in so many ways. Diana had already mended it three different times. How could she not be embarrassed of him?

And then she said the words he'd been longing to hear. "I love you, Kevin. You could never embarrass me."

Kevin smiled. "And I love you!"

THE JOURNEY BACK TO Wyoming was a quiet one, the rhythmic chugging of the train lulling both Kevin and Diana into contemplation. The future stretched before them, uncertain yet full of potential. As they disembarked at their destination, Kevin's hand found hers, their fingers intertwining for a brief moment that spoke volumes.

"Back to reality," he murmured, his voice tinged with wistfulness, as if leaving behind a dream.

"Reality isn't so bad," Diana replied, squeezing his hand before letting go. "We have each other, after all."

They arrived home, the familiar sight of the cabin a comforting anchor amidst the whirlwind of possibilities that swirled around them. Kevin wasted no time in returning to work, eager to keep his mind occupied while they awaited news from the medical school.

Diana, too, sought solace in the routine of life, turning her attention to the garden. It was springtime, and the earth felt alive beneath her fingers as she tended to the budding flowers and vegetables. She cherished these moments of peace, a connection to nature that grounded her even as her thoughts raced ahead.

"Diana!" Keri's voice cut through the quiet like a knife, and Diana looked up to see her friend running toward her, waving something above her head. "It's here!"

"Is that...?" Diana's heart caught in her throat, her trowel slipping from her grasp as she rose to her feet.

"Kevin's letter from the medical school!" Keri panted, her eyes wide with excitement as she handed it over. "One of the ranch hands brought it from town."

"Thank you, Keri," Diana said, her voice trembling slightly as she held the envelope in her hands. This simple piece of paper held the key to Kevin's dreams— and perhaps, to their future together.

"Go on, open it!" Keri urged, bouncing on her toes like an eager child.

"Shouldn't we wait for Kevin?" Diana hesitated, torn between her own curiosity and the desire to share this moment with her husband.

"All right," Keri agreed reluctantly. "But you better let me know as soon as he reads it!"

"I promise," Diana replied with a smile, clutching the letter to her chest as she watched Keri hurry back toward her house.

As she stood there in the garden, the sun warm on her face, Diana felt a surge of hope and anticipation. She knew that whatever the contents of the letter, their lives were about to change. And though she longed for the stability of love, she couldn't deny the thrill that coursed through her veins at the thought of leaping into the unknown—but it would be very different than the last time she'd done it. This time, Kevin would be at her side.

"Please," she whispered, her heart full to bursting as she held the key to their fate. "Let this be the beginning of something wonderful."

Diana was in the kitchen fixing supper, the envelope never out of her sight. She couldn't wait for Kevin to open it so they would know what was possible for their future.

"Kevin should be home soon," she mused, pausing to wipe sweat from her brow. Her heart fluttered with anticipation; her thoughts consumed by the contents of the envelope. She glanced down at it, her fingers itching to tear it open, but she resisted the urge—this was a moment they needed to share together.

The distant rumble of horse hooves reached Diana's ears, tearing her away from her thoughts. She looked up, her eyes scanning the horizon for any sign of Kevin's return. There he was, emerging from the tree line, riding atop his trusty steed, Thunder. A smile bloomed across her face, pure joy radiating through her.

She removed the stew pot from the middle of the stove, pushing it to the edge where it wouldn't burn before running outside to see him.

"Kevin!" she shouted, waving her arms to catch his attention. As he drew closer, she could see the lines of exhaustion etched across his handsome features, evidence of another hard day's work. His eyes sparkled as soon as they saw her, and she knew he cared for her just as much as she cared for him—even if they never said it.

"Hey there," he called, dismounting as he reached her side. "What's got you so excited?"

"Your letter arrived today," Diana said, holding out the envelope. "I wanted us to open it together."

"Thank you, sweetheart," Kevin replied, taking the letter from her trembling hands. He hesitated for a moment, stealing a glance at her face, as if searching for reassurance.

"Go ahead," she urged, her voice barely above a whisper. "We've waited long enough."

With a nod, Kevin broke the seal and unfolded the letter, scanning the words that would determine the course of their lives. A moment passed, then another, before his face lit up with elation.

"I...I got in, Diana! I've been accepted to medical school!" he stammered his voice thick with emotion.

Tears welled up in Diana's eyes, threatening to spill over as she wrapped her arms around him, burying her face in the crook of his neck. "Oh, Kevin, I'm so happy for you!"

"Thank you, sweetheart," he whispered, his breath warm against her ear. As they stood together, enveloped in each other's arms, Diana was struck by the enormity of the moment—of the dreams they were finally ready to chase.

"Are you sure about this?" she asked quietly, her voice barely audible above the gentle rustle of leaves. "Leaving the ranch, starting this new life?"

Kevin pulled back, his gaze meeting hers with a steadfast determination. "I think so. We'll have to look at what we want and make a final decision together."

"Can you believe it?" he whispered, disbelief still lacing his voice. "All this time, I thought it was just a dream, but now..."

Diana looked up at him, her eyes shining with unshed tears. "It's real, Kevin. And I couldn't be prouder of you."

He smiled down at her, his own eyes glistening. "Thank you, sweetheart." Then, after a moment's pause, he added, "But now I have to decide if medical school is really what I want."

His words took Diana by surprise, and she tilted her head in confusion. "What do you mean? I thought this was your dream?"

Kevin sighed, his eyes drifting toward the horizon as if searching for answers. "It was...or at least, I thought it was. But the ranch, the people here—they've become a part of me, too. And now I'm torn."

Diana bit her lip, considering his words. She knew how much he loved the ranch, the sense of belonging it had given him. But she also understood his desire to pursue a career in medicine—to make a difference in the world beyond the boundaries of their little corner of Wyoming.

"Whatever you decide, Kevin," she said softly, reaching up to brush a stray lock of hair from his forehead, "I'll be by your side, supporting you every step of the way."

"I know, Diana. I can't tell you how much that means to me."

"Whatever you choose, Kevin," she whispered, "I know it will be the right decision."

And with that, they stood hand in hand, watching as the sun dipped below the horizon—its warm, golden glow a promise of the future that awaited them, whatever it may hold.

Chapter Nine

Diana stood at the kitchen window, watching Kevin walk pensively across the yard, his shoulders tense and head bent. The vast Wyoming landscape stretched out before them, a testament to the life they had built together. It had been a week since their conversation about Kevin's future, and she couldn't help but worry as he grappled with the possibility of leaving ranching for four long years.

"Come sit down with me," Diana called as Kevin stepped through the door. He hesitated for a moment and then joined her at the small oak table, calloused hands gently clasping hers.

"Have you given more thought to what you want?" Diana asked softly, concern etched in her eyes. "You know I'll support you either way."

Kevin rubbed his thumb across the back of her hand, lost in thought. "I just don't know, Diana. Four years away from this place... That's a long time."

"Of course it is," she acknowledged, squeezing his hand reassuringly. "But listen, Kevin, if you'd rather keep working for the Whites, I'm fine with that. I love our life here. And if you'd rather have your own ranch, we can do that too. But if you want to be a doctor, now is the time." She saw the conflict in his eyes, the desire to pursue his dream of helping others battling with his deep-rooted love for the land and the life they had built together. Her heart ached for him, knowing that no matter what decision he made, there would be a part of him that felt unfulfilled.

"Let's take some time to think about it, all right?" Diana suggested, hoping to ease his burden. "We don't have to decide right this second."

"Thank you," Kevin said, his voice thick with emotion. He leaned over and pressed a soft kiss to her forehead, gratitude shining in his eyes. "I'm so lucky to have you."

"Likewise," Diana whispered, hugging him tightly.

"MORNING," KEVIN GREETED her as he stepped onto the porch, his own mug in hand. He eased into a chair beside her, his gaze following hers across the expanse of their world.

"Good morning" Diana replied softly. "I've been thinking about our conversation last week, about your options."

"Me too," Kevin admitted, rubbing at the back of his neck. "I've been considering what you said about moving to Aurora for medical school, then coming back here afterward. It'd be hard, being away from all this for so long, but I reckon it could work."

Diana took a deep breath, letting the crisp air fill her lungs as she mentally prepared herself for the conversation ahead. "We could buy a house there, something small and comfortable. Just for the four years while you're in school and doing your internship. Once it's over, we could move back here to Wyoming and start our new life together."

"Would you really be okay with leaving everything behind for four years?" Kevin asked, his eyes searching hers for any hint of doubt or reluctance.

Diana reached over and placed her hand on his, giving it a reassuring squeeze. "If it means supporting your dreams and making a better life for us, then yes, I'm more than willing to do it."

"Thank you, Diana," Kevin said, his voice choked with emotion. "I think... I think I want to go to medical school. When I imagine my future, I see myself helping people, and I can't shake that feeling. But I also want to come back here afterward, start a ranch of our own, and be the doctor for the area."

"Then that's what we'll do," Diana affirmed with a smile, her heart swelling with pride for the man she loved. "And I know it won't be easy, but we'll make it through together."

"Are you sure about this? It's a big change, and we'd be leaving Harry and Keri and everything we know behind for a while," Kevin said, his eyes reflecting both hope and fear.

"Life is full of changes," Diana mused. "We just have to embrace them and trust in God to carry us through. Besides, this place will always be here, waiting for us when we're ready to return."

Kevin looked out over the ranch, his gaze lingering on the rolling hills and distant mountains that had become such an integral part of his life. With a sigh, he turned back to Diana, determination shining in his eyes.

"All right. Let's do it. We'll move to Aurora, and then we'll come back here and build a new life together."

The sun dipped low in the sky, casting an orange glow over the ranch as laughter and music filled the air. Keri had outdone herself, transforming her home into a lively venue for Kevin and Diana's going away party.

"Can you believe it?" Diana mused, her eyes scanning the crowd of familiar faces gathered around them. "We're really leaving this place tomorrow."

"Change is inevitable," Kevin replied, wrapping an arm around her waist and pulling her closer. "Besides, I can see how excited you are for this new adventure."

"Of course I am!" she exclaimed, her heart swelling with pride for Kevin's decision to pursue his dream of becoming a doctor. "But I'll miss this place, and all the wonderful people we've come to know."

"You won't be gone forever," Harry chimed in, clapping Kevin on the back. "We'll be right here waiting for you when you get back. And who knows, maybe by then my Keri will have written enough mail-order bride romances that we can buy even more land!"

Keri rolled her eyes playfully at her husband's remark, but couldn't hide the affection in her smile. "Now that would be a plot twist," she quipped, joining the group with a tray of her homemade cookies.

As the evening wore on, the mood became bittersweet, with friends and family sharing stories and memories, laughter mingling with tears. Diana found herself torn between the excitement of their new life in Aurora and the ache of leaving behind the community they had grown to love.

"Diana," Kevin whispered in her ear as they swayed together during a slow dance, "I promise we'll make the most of our time away, and when we return, we'll build an even better life here."

Diana nodded, her eyes glistening with unshed tears. "I know we will," she murmured, her thoughts drifting to the secret she had kept from him—the land she had already purchased for their future ranch, waiting patiently for their return.

The night wore on, and eventually, it was time for goodbyes. As they hugged and kissed their friends, Diana felt a mixture of sadness, pride, and anticipation coursing through her veins. This was the first chapter of their new life together, and she couldn't wait to see where it would lead them.

"Goodbye, everyone!" Kevin called out, his voice strong but tinged with emotion. "We'll be back before you know it!"

"Take care of each other," Keri whispered to Diana as they embraced one last time. "And remember, this isn't the end. It's just the beginning."

Diana nodded, drawing strength from Keri's words. With a final wave, she climbed into the wagon, most of their belongings set to be sent on after they left.

Chapter Ten

Diana's days were much lonelier when they arrived in Aurora, and she was thrilled to find a church there where she could spend time with other people.

As soon as Kevin got home, he would eat whatever she'd fixed for supper, and then he'd go into the study they'd set up in one of the rooms of their small three-bedroom house there in Colorado.

"Another late night, huh?" Diana asked, concern furrowing her brow as she watched him sit at the desk, his eyes scanning the pages before him.

"Looks like it," Kevin replied, his eyes not leaving the textbook. "I want to finish this chapter before I turn in."

Diana knew how hard he was working and couldn't help but admire his dedication. This new life together came with its challenges, but she could see the determination in Kevin's eyes, fueled by a desire to make a difference in the world.

"All right, I'll leave you to it," she said with a warm smile. "Just remember to get some sleep, okay?"

"Promise," he murmured, his eyes already back on the pages before him.

As Diana turned to head back into the bedroom, she felt a flutter in her heart— a feeling that had become all too familiar over the past months. She knew that Kevin's late nights studying would pay off one day, and as she settled into bed, she couldn't help but think of the bright future they were building together.

The snow fell gently outside the window, casting a serene glow on the world, while inside, Diana's heart weighed heavy with loneliness.

The flickering flames in the fireplace provided a comforting warmth, but couldn't fill the void left by Kevin's absence.

"Maybe I shouldn't have pressed him so hard to pursue his dreams," she thought, folding her hands in her lap. "Is it wrong for me to want more of his attention?"

"Diana, are you okay?" Kevin asked, looking up from his textbook, concern etched on his face.

"Of course," she responded, forcing a smile and brushing away the stray tears that threatened to fall. "I'm just feeling a little emotional, that's all."

"Let me put this away and keep you company," he offered, closing the book and standing up, but she quickly shook her head.

"No, don't," she insisted. "You need to study, and I know how important this is for our future. I'll be fine, really."

"Are you sure?" Kevin questioned, his eyes searching hers for any sign of hesitation.

"Absolutely. Go on, get back to it." She mustered a reassuring grin, even as her heart ached for the simple closeness they had shared before his studies consumed his time.

"All right, if you say so," he relented, returning to his desk. She watched him for a moment, wondering if they would ever find their way back to each other amidst the sea of medical jargon that now filled their days.

A few days later, just before Christmas, Diana found herself in the office of a doctor there in Aurora. "I don't know what's wrong with me," she said. "I'm so tired all the time, and I'm hungry. But I throw up anything I eat before noon. But I still eat because I'm so hungry. I don't even make sense to myself anymore."

The doctor smiled. "And your cycles?"

She frowned, her brows drawing together. "Well, I haven't had one since we've come to Aurora, but I thought it was just that our lives were upended."

"Are your clothes getting tighter?" he asked.

She nodded slowly. "I'm expecting!"

The doctor smiled and nodded. "I'll give you the name of a good midwife in town. Make sure you continue to eat well, and don't worry. Your baby is going to be fine."

When she got home, she knew it was just after Kevin arrived home from school. As she walked in the door, she called his name, "Kevin!" she called, her voice shaking with emotion. "Kevin, I need you!"

"Is everything okay?" he asked into the living room where she stood.

She nodded. "I haven't been feeling well, so I went to see Dr. Ochoa. He was recommended by some friends from church. And...I'm pregnant!"

Kevin's eyes widened with excitement. "Really?"

"Yes, we're going to have a baby," she confirmed, tears of joy streaming down her cheeks.

"Wow, I can hardly believe it." He pulled her close, their hearts beating in sync as they shared the news that would forever change their lives. "I promise, I'll be there for you and our baby, no matter what."

"Just finish medical school before he or she is born. I'm going to need you close."

He embraced her tenderly. "A baby. I guess I need to start reading up on obstetrics."

She laughed. "We have a few months yet. The doctor thinks beginning of June."

"It seems like it's too soon and not soon enough."

Diana stood watching Kevin as he studied for his first semester exams. He looked so tired. "Long day?" she asked, as she rubbed his neck, knowing it would make him feel better. He spent too many hours hunched over his school books.

Kevin looked up at her, forcing a smile. "Very. One more day of exams, and I have a few weeks off."

"Can I get you anything? Coffee, tea?" Diana offered, hoping to ease his burden in any way she could.

"Tea would be great, thanks." He sighed, running a hand through his hair. "I just don't know if I can keep this up for another semester, Diana. It's so much harder than I thought it would be."

"You're doing an amazing job," she reassured him, moving to the kitchen to prepare his drink. She glanced back at him, taking in his slouched shoulders and defeated expression. "You've come so far already, Kevin. And I believe in you."

"Thanks," he murmured, his voice thick with emotion.

As she brought him his tea, Diana felt a strong kick from the baby within her. The force of it startled her, causing her to pause and place a hand on her belly.

"Wow," she breathed, looking down at the spot where she'd felt the movement. "Baby's getting stronger. I can't believe I was expecting for so long without realizing it."

He smiled. "The human body is absolutely amazing. I can't wait to hold him in my arms."

"Her," Diana corrected, smiling. "I'm having a girl."

He smiled at her constant reminders of the baby being a girl. "I can't believe we're going to be parents soon."

"Neither can I," she admitted, her heart swelling with love for the man standing beside her and the child growing within her. "But I know we'll be amazing at it."

"I promise I'll do everything I can to provide for us," Kevin vowed, his eyes sincere as they met hers. "I just hope I can get through the next semester without falling apart."

"Have faith in yourself," Diana urged gently, placing a hand on his cheek. "I do."

"Thank you," he whispered, leaning into her touch. "For believing in me and for being my rock."

"Always," she promised, her heart full of love and determination.

The sun had barely risen and the sky was a canvas of soft pinks and purples as Diana sat in the kitchen, her hands gripping the edge of the table. The pain had started as a dull ache earlier that morning, but now it came in waves, each one stronger than the last.

"Are you sure you don't want me to call the doctor? Or the midwife?" Kevin asked, his voice thick with worry as he stood beside her, his hand hovering uncertainly over her shoulder.

"You have your graduation today," she reminded him through gritted teeth, her eyes squeezed shut as another contraction rippled through her body. "I can't ask you to miss that. I'm not having this baby until it's done."

"I don't care about walking across the stage," Kevin insisted, his eyes never leaving her face. "You and the baby are more important to me. I'll stay here with you."

"Kevin, please," she managed to gasp out between contractions. "You've worked so hard for this. You deserve to be recognized for your achievements."

He hesitated for a moment, torn between his desire to be there for Diana and the culmination of all his hard work at school. But as he looked into her eyes, filled with pain and determination, he knew there was only one choice he could make.

"All right," he agreed, swallowing hard. "But as soon as I get back, I'm calling Dr. Thompson, all right? Promise me you'll hang in there until then."

"Promise," she whispered, a small smile crossing her lips despite the pain.

The moment Kevin's name was called at his graduation, he sped home, diploma clutched tightly in his hand. Bursting through the front door, he found Diana on the floor of their bedroom, her breathing ragged and uneven.

"I'm here," he said urgently, dropping to his knees beside her. "I'll help you through this."

"Kevin, it's happening so fast," she gasped, the fear in her eyes making him ache with worry.

"Stay calm," he instructed, trying to keep his voice steady as he took her hand. "We can do this together."

And so they did, with Kevin guiding Diana through each contraction, holding her hand tight and murmuring words of encouragement. Hours later, when their baby finally entered the world, Kevin couldn't help but feel that this moment was more significant than any graduation ceremony could have been.

"Look, we did it," he whispered in awe as he cradled their newborn daughter in his arms. "We're parents."

"Thanks to you," she replied, exhaustion and gratitude etched into every line of her face. "You were amazing."

Two weeks later, Kevin began his internship with Dr. Thompson, a kind-hearted local doctor who had been instrumental in helping him get through school. As he walked into the small clinic for the first time, he carried with him the memory of bringing his child into the world—a moment that had forever changed him.

"Morning, Kevin," Dr. Thompson greeted him with a warm smile. "Ready to dive in?"

"More than ready, sir," Kevin replied, determination and excitement coursing through him. He knew he had much to learn, but he was eager to embrace this new chapter in his life.

As he set about his work, he couldn't help but think of Diana and their daughter, Caroline, back at home, waiting for him. They were his motivation, his reason for pushing forward and becoming the man they both needed him to be.

A month later, Diana sat in her rocking chair, nursing the baby and reading a letter from Keri, whom she missed dearly. Sure, she'd made other friends, but none quite so special as Keri.

My Dearest Diana,

As the sun sets over our beloved Wyoming, I find myself seated at our old wooden table, pen in hand. The warmth of the hearth is comforting, but your words, carried across the miles by the whispering winds, bring a different kind of warmth—one that fills the heart with joy and longing.

Firstly, let me extend my heartfelt congratulations to Kevin. His achievement is indeed a testament to his determination and unwavering dedication. To think that he is now a doctor, ready to heal and serve, fills me with immense pride. Even from this distance, I can almost see the sparkle in his eyes, the humble pride of a man who has worked tirelessly toward his dream.

How wonderful it must be, dear Diana, to be the partner of such a remarkable man! I remember when he first shared his dreams of attending medical school. Today, those dreams are a reality, and I couldn't be happier for both of you. He will surely make a great difference in the lives of those he serves, just as he has in ours.

Here in Wyoming, life carries on with its usual rhythm. The cattle are faring well, and the crops are promising a good yield. Harry sends his regards. He often speaks fondly of the times he spent working with Kevin. We both miss you dearly.

But the news that has truly warmed my heart is the arrival of little Caroline. Oh, how I long to hold her in my arms, to see her tiny fingers curl around mine. I am certain she is as beautiful and radiant as her mother. Being a mother is a blessing, Diana, and I know you will embrace this new journey with all the love and grace that you possess. I cannot wait until our children can play together. My son, Albert, is looking forward to meeting his future wife, Caroline. He is doing well, and growing much too quickly for his mother's taste.

As I conclude this letter, allow me to express my deepest joy and happiness for all the blessings that life has bestowed upon you. Kevin's accomplishment, the birth of your lovely daughter Caroline, the love and warmth that envelops your home—these are treasures, Diana, to be cherished and celebrated.

I eagerly await your letters, filled with tales of motherhood and the adventures of Dr. Kevin. Until then, know that you are in my thoughts and prayers. May the winds of Wyoming carry my love and best wishes to you and your beautiful family in Colorado.

With all my heart,

Keri

THREE YEARS LATER, Diana and Kevin took the train back to Wyoming with their two children, Caroline, and Thomas. Kevin still didn't know about the land she'd purchased before leaving Wyoming, and she wanted it to be her graduation gift to Kevin.

He was still adamant that he wanted to be a rancher as well as a doctor, and she'd commissioned a house to be built on the land, with an attached doctor's office. She'd leave the purchasing of his cattle to Kevin, but she'd made sure there was a bunkhouse, so the men who worked for them would have a place to lay their heads.

Best of all, the land was adjacent to Harry and Keri's land, and their homes would still be a five-minute distance apart.

Soon, they were in a wagon and headed out to their new land. Kevin never asked where they should go, he simply started out toward the

Whites' ranch, and Diana didn't say a word. She would tell him at the Whites and they would all enjoy his reaction together.

Diana was surprised at the party awaiting them at the Whites' to welcome them home to Wyoming.

Many different people wanted to toast Kevin, the new doctor in the area. Finally, after all who wished to speak had welcomed them home, Diana spoke up. "This will come as a surprise to some of you, but Kevin had a very hard time deciding if he wanted to be a rancher or a doctor, and we settled on both. He is now a doctor ready to put out his shingle, but I've purchased the land for our ranch, and a house has been built on it as my graduation gift to him." She turned to her husband. "Kevin, you amaze me a little more every day, and I'm so proud to call you my husband."

Kevin stood slack jawed for a moment before embracing her. "I just hope it's close to here."

Diana looked over at Keri. "Would you mind my children for a few minutes?"

At Keri's nod, Diana took Kevin's hand, and led him from the house and toward their new home. "It's a nice big house, and we'll fill it with our children, but I also had an office made for you attached to the house. I thought it would make things easier for you as you juggle being a doctor with ranching."

As they walked through the house, he shook his head. "Diana, I don't know what I've done to deserve you, but it must have been something tremendous." He went into the office before going to the house, thrilled that he could see the Whites' house from his office.

"This is perfect. You thought of everything!" He pulled her to him and kissed her softly. "I love you with everything inside of me. Thank you for making my dreams come true."

Diana shook her head. "You made your dreams come true. I just helped a little bit along the way."